Disclaimer

Billionaire Romance

The Billionaire's Private Island

Billionaire Island Romance Series
Book 3

By Alessandra Bancroft

Table of Contents

Chapter 1: The Billionaire's Beauties

"Glad that's finally over," Luke said to Petra with a sigh. While it was true that he was handsome, successful, smart, respected and a billionaire, he'd still had a bad case of nerves telling five of the ten women he'd had brought to his tropical paradise to go home. Sure, the girls all knew about each other – now – but he'd expected tears and tantrums.

Petra snorted derisively, spinning her chair to face the screens filled with video feed of the five girls returning to their mansions. "Over? Hardly. What's your itinerary for picking two out of the five you've kept?"

Luke looked at the screens thoughtfully. Any of these beautiful women would look amazing on his arm out in society, and he was pretty sure they'd steam up his nights as well, but only *one* of them would be the perfect companion with which to build his empire. He shook his head and concentrated. First he needed to narrow the field down to two.

"I had fun with Pamela. Maybe something relaxing? A day exploring the caves on the South end of the island? She's an archeologist, she'd like that," Luke said, recalling that the cave in question had a sandy floor perfect for a romantic picnic, and then hopefully some of the delightful British woman for dessert.

Petra shook her head. "A bit ordinary if you ask me."

Luke glared at his assistant. "I didn't. Just set it up. Tell her to dress casual."

Petra rolled her eyes but dialed Pamela's house phone anyway. As she started getting everything together, Luke headed off for the gym. Maybe Sergio would approve heavier weights today since his back had been feeling much better since Yuna had worked her magic on it. He grinned at the memory. Yuna had magic in her hands, but her real spell was between those glorious thighs. He could still hear her beautiful voice in his ear... begging him to take it slow. He grinned, reliving the experience in his head once again.

###

"He did not name you first. You are not first in his mind!" Helga inspected Svetlana head to toe, circling her, and eyeing every garment.

"I am well aware," Svetlana snapped at her ex-KGB matchmaker. "But I will be. Rest assured."

"The only thing I am *assured* of is that the organization will not tolerate failure. This is not one of your petty little millionaires, Svetlana. A multi-billionaire wants only the *best* – and that you must be!" Helga dealt a vicious pinch to Svetlana's upper arm, nodding briskly when the younger woman didn't flinch.

Svetlana eyed her coldly, adjusting the sleeves on her linen dress. "I have plans. None of them involves failure. Now, if you'll excuse me, I believe I'll pay a little visit," she said.

Chapter 2: Pamela and the Picnic

"I think it's quite nice of Svetlana to invite us to dinner," Catherine, Pamela's matchmaker, said.

"I think she's a viper in Chanel clothing, but I'm not going to miss a chance to find out what she's up to," Pamela said. She touched her hair to make sure it was still in place despite the brisk evening breeze.

Svetlana's mansion was identical to her own as far as Pamela could tell, with the slight exception of the terrorized desperation on the faces of the servants. *"Well,"* she thought, *"at least I'm right thinking the woman's a horror."*

"So good of you to join us," Svetlana said. Her voice was a low, sultry purr that had Pamela's hackles rising.

"Thank you for having us," Catherine chirped, seemingly oblivious to the undercurrents in the room.

"You are both most welcome. Come, we'll talk. Perhaps you could give me an idea of what to discuss with such a commanding, domineering, and intellectual man – I'm rather at a loss, I must admit," Svetlana said.

"I've really been looking forward to this," Luke said, smiling down at Pamela when she opened the door.

"Me too!" Pamela's eyes were wide and sparkling and he couldn't help but dip his head to kiss her hello.

He tucked one long golden strand of hair behind her ear, and then took her hand in his own. "I hope you're up for a picnic," he said.

"That sounds wonderful," she said smiling at him. She gave his hand a squeeze and cuddled up to his arm as they walked towards the limousine for the short drive.

Luke looked down at her head resting on his arm, then straight forward again, an irrepressible grin on his face. She definitely wasn't wearing a bra. He was pretty sure that his chances of having the little professor for dessert just went up significantly.

He held the door open and watched her slide across the leather bench seat in a skirt much shorter than the Bermuda shorts he'd last seen her in. His eyes followed the length of her legs all the way up... *"No panties* and *no bra,"* he thought as his gaze continued upwards to her nipples pebbled under the silk blouse that clung to her curves.

Their eyes met, and she gave him a slow, sexy smile, then beckoned him, crooking a finger and giving him a wink. He dove into the limousine, slapping the button to raise up the black glass between the driver and them.

"Hello again," Pamela said, her voice low and sultry as she wrapped her arms around his neck and drew him in for a scorching kiss.

Luke briefly thought that this was strange behavior from her, considering how sweetly shy she had been on the yacht, but shrugged and went with it. Who was he to question good fortune?

He slipped first one hand, then the other under the back of her blouse, reveling in the feel of her smooth skin under his hands. She reached behind her and took his left hand and put it on her breast. He felt it up thoroughly and then began to flick his thumb across her nipple.

"Mmm. Nice. Pinching's good too," she said, then proceeded to nibble on the side of his neck while impatiently tugging his polo shirt out of his pants. She straddled his lap while trying to unbuckle his belt, which made the process a bit awkward, but at that point she was rocking her hips against his erection and he didn't care if she was clumsy or not.

"Fuck me," Pamela ordered once she had his pants undone and pulled down, both hands gripping his cock just barely on the good side of too tight. Luke didn't like being bossed around, especially when it came to sex. He grabbed a large tuft of her long curly hair then slowly pushed her head down. She moved back in the large limousine and got on her knees, looking up at him as she gave him one long, slow lick along his entire length. Luke's eyes widened at the sight and he groaned in pleasure. "Jackpot!" he thought as she spent the next minute licking him sexily. "Give it to me baby!" Pamela said again forcefully, as she seductively sucked the tip of his shaft.

"I will. Because I want to," Luke said, lifting her up and gently rubbing his penis up and down her dripping wet pussy.

Her eyes widened and her mouth fell open. She whimpered and clutched his shoulders so hard he could feel her nails digging into him through his shirt. He held her hips absolutely still and then bucked upwards into her. She tried to grind into him when he hit bottom, but he was too big and she wasn't warmed up yet.

"I don't take orders," he said, looking into Pamela's eyes for a long moment before she stopped her desperate attempts for more contact. She bit her lip to stifle a needy whimper and nodded. At that, he ground against her, making her keen and lean into him, her mouth caressing his shoulder.

Luke stopped bucking, leaned back, and slid his hands up her sides. He let her ride him as she pleased while removing the blouse blocking his view of her luscious breasts. She rode him faster, mewling.

He rode out her first orgasm with his jaw clenched, determined to hold out. Pamela collapsed against him and he rubbed her back for a few minutes, rocking gently against her but not allowing himself to get over-excited just yet. When she started to respond to his touch again he reversed their positions on the limousine's bench seat without pulling out of her sweet depths, kneeling on the lushly carpeted floor with a very satisfied looking Pamela on her back.

Luke moved her legs, putting both over one of his shoulders. He slipped a hand between them to rest his thumb against her clit, then leaned forward to brace his weight on the backs of her thighs and his other hand. She looked a little unsure until he started thrusting into her. She gasped, crossed her ankles, and bent her knees trying to pull him in even closer.

Luke grinned, driving into her harder and faster until she screamed, scrabbling at his ass with her nails, trying desperately to somehow get more of him. He sped up, reveling in the sights and sounds of bringing her to completion, finally grunting with the force of his own orgasm as Pamela bucked and moaned in ultimate pleasure. Luke grabbed her breasts as she milked every last drop from him, panting, and trying to recover. After a minute he gave her a juicy kiss then pushed himself upright, slipping from her.

"Wow," Pamela said when she finally got her breath back and presence of mind enough to speak.

"Yeah," Luke said, pleased with himself and with her. His ass had more stripes than that damned cereal box tiger, and he was pretty sure that he was bleeding in several spots.

"That was fun! We should eat that picnic now, though," Pamela said. She sat forward and plucked her blouse off of the limousine floor and popped it back over her head. "We need to keep our strength up," she said with one last squeeze of his butt.

"Yeah," he replied, a little nonplussed by her sudden bright perkiness. He had a nearly insatiable libido and even *he* wasn't jumping up and wanting a sandwich!

Chapter 3: Snorkeling with Kiko

"Ugh! It was more like a fucking power struggle than sex," Luke told Petra that night when he finally returned. "It would be great if she was *really* that insatiable, but I swear she was in *pain* by the third time around and wouldn't admit it. It was crazy."

"Three words. Too. Much. Information," Petra said, holding up three fingers.

"Well, you *did* ask how it went. If she's like that all the time she's *definitely* not the one. It was a battle! She *bit* me. I have *blood stains on my ass from where she scratched me.* Scratching is okay, mauling is *not*," he said, shaking his head. "You know how I get when people mess with me too much!"

Petra laughed and pointed to a few extra dots of blood he hadn't noticed on his neck, then said, "Well, you're snorkeling with Kiko tomorrow, and she doesn't seem like the blood thirsty type."

Luke rolled his eyes and headed off to disinfect his wounds, grumbling as Petra's continued giggles and comments about 'man meat' followed him down the hallway.

"I told you it would work. One down, three to go," Svetlana said, smiling at her matchmaker.

"I still want to know how you knew she wouldn't trust you and would try to dominate him," Helga said, eyes narrowing at Svetlana as she removed the earpiece from her ear.

"The same way I know Kiko *will* trust me. You can't do what I do if you don't study people," Svetlana said.

"What will you tell her?"

"Why, that he can't stand intellectual discussions and prefers women who are extremely shy, childlike, and prudish, of course." Svetlana smiled with malicious glee.

###

"I don't think this bathing suit covers enough," Kiko told her matchmaker early the next afternoon.

Kaito looked her up and down with a wry twist to her lips. "It covers more than the bathing suit I wore for swim class when I was a girl. I'm more concerned that it undoes whatever good wearing that push up bra did on your first date with Mr. Garmount."

"Svetlana said he seemed displeased with her age, and she's only a month older than I am. I won't pander to perversion, but I can definitely look younger than *she* does. I'm sure all that frowning will give her ghastly wrinkles," Kiko said, smiling impishly while she braided her hair.

Kaito tried to remain solemn, but her lip twitched and soon both of them were giggling. "That Svetlana, she thinks she's so very smart and sophisticated. She can't possibly compare to you, my dear," Kaito said.

###

Luke refused to let this date go poorly. He still remembered the one sweet kiss he'd gotten from Kiko and didn't intend that to be the last he had of her.

12

He threw a linen camp shirt and chino shorts on over his bathing suit and had the staff pack a basket with snorkeling gear for both of them, towels for drying off and much bigger ones to sunbathe on – or, hopefully, much more. He smiled, fantasizing vividly about Kiko writhing beneath him on the sun-warmed sand.

When Kiko opened the door he met her eyes for a long moment before she turned her head and lowered her eyes, blushing charmingly. His eyes widened as he took in her outfit. Luke thought the blouse was cute, but he wasn't sure skirts that short were even a thing outside of porn. He definitely didn't mind.

"You look *amazing*," he said, then reached out and tried to hug her. She squirmed away, looking over her shoulder at Kaito. He was a little annoyed, that reticence about public touching really killed any kind of spontaneity.

"Thank you," she said. "You look very handsome too." She smiled up at him briefly before looking away.

The ride over to the cove he'd picked out for snorkeling was short but pleasant. They discussed the application of Kiko's alloys in the computer industry, and he delighted in the way her face lit up when talking about her own field of expertise.

She ducked modestly behind a bush to change when they arrived. He smiled, imagining her in one of the string bikinis he'd seen the girls wearing during their get-togethers, then pictured peeling her out of her bathing suit under the cove's waterfall.

He saw just her hands as she draped her blouse and skirt over the bush. He stripped off his own clothing and tossed them in the general direction of a nearby bush. He kicked off his shoes and retrieved the basket, trying to talk himself out of the erection he had just thinking about her nearly naked behind that bush.

Kiko emerged and his jaw all but dropped. That was definitely not what he had been expecting. She was wearing a suit that looked like a nightmare combination of a school uniform and the bathing suits his great-grandmother wore in the 1930s. It was navy blue and flattened what had been small but pleasant curves into a distinctly flat and boyish shape. The hard-on he'd been battling in anticipation gave up.

Oblivious to his dismay, she gave a little twirl and took the snorkeling gear in her size from the basket and actually *skipped* toward the water with the flippers in her hand. He sighed and joined her, determined to at least get *through* the date, but all thoughts of peeling her out of her swimsuit had thoroughly died.

Chapter 4: Dova's Run

"She looked like a fucking twelve-year-old. Of *course* nothing happened," Luke snarled at Petra over sandwiches in the kitchen. "And she was acting nothing like the woman I met on our first date on the beach under the moonlight."

"Yeah. About that. Svetlana's been going around to the other girls and messing with their heads," Petra said, somehow managing to eat a thick Reuben daintily.

Luke held up a finger, chewing on his own bite of roast beef sandwich, then swallowed, a sour grimace on his face. Luke's voice became much harsher as he said, "She was gullible enough to fall for whatever it was Svetlana said, *and* she freaked out when I tried to hug her in front of *one* person – can you imagine what the tabloids would make of that?"

"Ugh. They'd paint her as some sort of cold, heartless bitch and try to trip her up every chance they got," she agreed. "Well, you've still got three more dates before you have to narrow it down."

"Exactly," said Luke, his voice softening as he thought of Dova. "Dova next, I think. She's a marathon runner – it might be nice to have my run across the island trails with some company tomorrow morning," Luke said.

"Better her than me, boss man. You set a punishing pace," Petra said ruefully.

Svetlana beckoned her matchmaker to follow her onto the trails, stripping off her white jacket to reveal the long-sleeved black tee she wore. She dug through the pockets of the jacket to pull out a long length of fine black gauze and black gloves.

"What are you planning?" Helga asked her charge, crossing her arms over her chest.

Svetlana shushed the older woman and pointed to a hammock nearby. "You stand here and pretend to converse with me as I relax in the evening shade. A small storm is approaching, perhaps an *accident* is in order."

Helga beamed with pride. "Ah! Now you finally think like KGB," she said.

Svetlana frowned. "That's what I'm afraid of," she said. She donned the gloves and wrapped the long gauze over her distinctive platinum hair and pale skin, uncoiling a long wire saw from her wrist as she melted into the shadows of the trees.

"I had the trails put in for my own runs, but I thought you might enjoy them too. The Comrades marathon is quite a bit more grueling, of course, but I'm sure you want to stay in condition," Luke said, smiling at Dova as he stretched before their run. Her sports mesh tank top and shorts were tiny and he was definitely enjoying the view.

"Thank you. Two bronze, six silvers, and two golds so far – my times have been good enough that I like to think someday I might win," Dova replied, though she seemed more serious about stretching than actually paying attention. Luke thought that this run looked to be his best ever when she bent over to touch her toes, straightened, and then jogged in place a little.

"Once around the island and then lunch?"

Dova only nodded in response, then set off at a steady, ground-eating pace. Luke blinked and rushed to catch up with her. He didn't like that. He wanted to start the race himself under his own conditions when he was fully warmed up... which he wasn't. Dova looked at him from the corner of her eye and tilted her head proudly, then sped up a little more. He sped up to match her pace, which was still a quite bit slower than his usual. She laughed and sped up again, and the race was on.

They ran down the western side of the island and across the southern tip, enjoying the exhilaration of the run and the beautiful scenery, though both were running too fast for easy conversation. As they continued up the eastern side of the island, the path abruptly became an obstacle course.

Dova hurdled over the downed leaves, trees, and branches, as did Luke, though he seethed at the condition his groundskeepers had allowed the path to get into – the storm last night had *not* been bad enough to cause this kind of damage.

Dova was just ahead of him when he saw her foot catch on a palm tree across the path. She let out a scream of surprise, hitting the ground with her hands and knees before tumbling forward.

Luke raced to her side with a burst of speed he didn't know he had in him. "Are you all right?"

Dova's hands were badly scratched and left bloody handprints on her leg as she checked her freely bleeding knees. She looked up at him with tears in her big brown eyes. "It hurts," she gasped as she grasped at her right knee.

"Is anything broken?" he asked, half-panicked that this would be like the accident that had ripped Carla from his life.

"I... I don't think so."

"Let's get you to Sergio," he said, picking her up. She was heavier than she looked, but still a featherweight compared to the weights he lifted every other day.

He held her close to his chest as she whimpered from the pain. "He'll fix you right up, Dova."

She reached up to hold onto his neck as he hurried along the path and nodded against his cheek. He hurried down the path as best he could, stepping over the fallen limbs and then noting, with a grim fury, the perfect cuts made through the trees and branches. "*What the fuck!*" he thought, ready to fire his groundskeeper on the spot.

He looked up at the branches overhead. Several more hung from mere splinters and he picked up his speed to a near jog, causing Dova to whimper again. "I'm sorry, but we're not out of the woods yet."

She looked at him with distaste at his terrible pun, but her look quickly changed to alarm when he jerked his head upwards at the threatening branches. "Please, Luke, hurry!" Dova wound her arms tighter around his neck, adjusting herself to rest her cheek against his neck. She clenched her jaw as he started loping forward in a run when a branch crashed to the path just behind them.

He took the first left-hand path heading towards his mansion in the center of the island and found no further damage to the trees, much to his relief. What he saw at the end of the trail closest to his home lit the fires of rage within him. A wire saw, coiled around itself to resemble a decorative bracelet, sparkled in the morning sunshine on the low dry-laid stone wall terrace.

Chapter 5: A Taste of Svetlana

"Two things – is she going to be okay, and who the *fuck* on this island is trying to kill me?" Luke demanded of Petra, Sergio, Sven, and Maximillian that afternoon after he had fully screamed at and interrogated his groundskeeper and found him to be innocent.

Sergio scratched the back of his head. "I checked her over and I don't think anything's broken. She's in real pain, but she still has a full range of movement, although she may have seriously sprained her knee. She should be able to run in the next Comrades Marathon, which was her main concern," he said.

Luke nodded. "Now. Which one of those crazy bitches is trying to kill me, and why the *hell* did they get so close?" said Luke, glaring at his bodyguards Sven and Maximillian.

"There's no way to tell. They all have alibis, with footage to prove it," Sven said, shaking his head. "I don't think they were trying for you, though – I think they're trying to eliminate the competition."

"I think you need to call this off before someone *does* get seriously hurt," Maximillian said. Luke sneered at his massive bodyguard, who was a good friend but who apparently still didn't truly understand who Luke was and is.

Luke laughed... an imperious laugh filled with the confidence of youth and power. He looked Maximillian directly in his blue eyes and stated in a powerful tone: "I want whoever has done this caught, turned over to the authority, and charged." Luke looked away then grumbled, "There is always a price to pay... and God knows by now... I am willing to pay it!"

Luke turned to Petra and she immediately knew that look. The look of a lord who had just been pushed too far... She tried her best to put on an encouraging smile as Luke turned to her. "Who's next on the agenda?" he asked.

Svetlana was a vision in a modestly draped white satin gown when she stepped from her doorway. Luke was briefly at a loss for words at her beauty, and even more so when she embraced him and kissed his cheeks.

"You are an absolute vision," he said, shaking his head in awe when he finally recovered enough to speak.

"Thank you, darling – you look delectable in that suit. It rather flatters your broad shoulders and trim waist," Svetlana replied, linking arms with him and pressing against him.

He smiled at her, though it didn't feel quite genuine, until he handed her into the limousine and saw that her dress, so demure from the front, was backless and cut so low that it was only a whisper above exposing her ass to his very appreciative eyes. There was no way in hell she was wearing panties under that. He just *had* to find a way to get this cold, distant woman to notice him!

"I hate to see you go, but oh, baby, do I ever love to watch you walk away," Luke quipped with a dazed and crooked smile.

Svetlana beamed up at him and laughed, low and throaty. "You are so funny! I'm glad that you have a sense of humor," she said.

He beamed at her as he climbed into the limo. *"Who knew the Ice Queen liked cornball humor?"* he thought, marveling at his luck in finding something to finally make her smile at him. "You *liked* that? I've got a million of 'em," he said.

"Of course I did! I'm not *all* business," she said, leaning towards him and purring softly into his ear.

He slipped an arm around her and tucked her against his side, enjoying the feel of her against him. "I thought we'd have dinner on the yacht tonight," he said. "It's moored at the pier I had built on the northern side of the island."

"That sounds lovely," she said. She didn't sound enthused, so Luke scrambled for something to bring back her good mood.

"We can talk about the Russian stock market if you'd like," he offered.

Svetlana patted his chest. "No, no. Let's not talk business tonight. What do you like best about your boat?"

"Right now? I like that I can be alone with the beautiful woman beside me," Luke said smiling. The limousine stopped at the pier and he got out and held the door open for her, reaching in to offer a hand to help her out.

She laughed again and gave her hips a sexy little shimmy to adjust her dress. "I'll look forward to that," she said, giving him a sultry look. They walked to the yacht, her arm threaded through his, reminding him with every step that she wasn't wearing a bra or panties.

He touched her side gently to help her balance on the stairs up to the boat, reveling in the silk of her skin and the glide of the satin of her gown under his hand. Once she was safely aboard, Luke followed her, thankful that his suit jacket was long enough to cover the evidence of his arousal. *Definitely curves under that dress... She looks so damned good I want to taste her,"* he thought.

Instead of heading towards the sumptuously laid table, Svetlana turned to face him and wrapped her arms around his neck. She leaned into him, crushing her large buxom breasts against him. "Are we alone enough yet?" she asked as Svetlana gazed into his eyes then playfully nibbled on his left ear.

"Yes. Definitely yes," he murmured, pulling her close and kissing her. She followed his lead and kissed him back, curling her fingers into his shoulders, and standing on tip-toes to get closer and tease him with her tongue.

Ignoring his surroundings, Luke walked her backward into the lavish cabin at the front of the yacht, kicking the door closed behind them. She pulled back three steps, breaking the kiss, and eased the shoulders of her gown forward and pulled her arms out the back, watching him with half-lidded eyes as she let go of the gown. It slithered to her feet, leaving her in only her shoes.

Luke moved forward, quickly meeting her as she stepped out of the satin puddle, crushing her to him and kissing her fiercely. She was perfection. This was his chance to claim the most beautiful woman in the world as his! His hands roamed over her alabaster skin, loving the feel of her soft breasts against his chest. She slid her hands under his suit jacket, easily dropping it to the floor. Svetlana eyed Luke appreciatively, enjoying his wide shoulders and muscled chest.

It wasn't even twenty seconds before Svetlana had Luke and herself fully naked, with nothing but a huge raging hard on between them, which Svetlana held in her right hand while French kissing Luke passionately. She then dropped to her knees in front of him. Seeing this gorgeous woman running her tongue around the head of his cock while looking up at him submissively made Luke crazy with desire. He moaned in delight as she licked along his length, and then sucked him nearly all the way down to his base while moving her tongue against him.

She took her time, teasing him repeatedly, getting him close, and then backing off. Her tongue was doing miraculous things and he didn't want to stop her, but he was nearly twitching with the need to cum. When he moved to just pick her up and toss her on the bed and fuck her senseless, she surprised him by taking him deep into her throat and swallowing convulsively, humming contentedly and looking up to watch the look on his face.

His eyes rolled back and he grunted, burying his hands in her hair and slamming his hips forward once, twice, three times... twenty times before coming hard. She backed off slightly, still swallowing and sucking, making him feel like lightning was loose in his veins. She didn't stop... she sucked out every last drop even as she dribbled out the corners of her mouth for a full minute afterwards. Luke was in heaven. "Finally!" Luke thought. "Finally a woman who knows how to give the supreme blow job!"

Svetlana sat back on her heels, licking her lips and looking up at him. "Mmmm. Salty. Like good caviar," she said as she took a sip of champagne to swallow down the contents in her mouth. She stood up and scooped her gown off of the floor behind her.

"Oh, no, none of that now," he said, picking her up and tossing her gown aside. He then brought her to the king-sized bed. "Turnabout is definitely fair play, and I definitely want a taste of *you*."

Chapter 6: Dancing with Yuna

"You should eat, you're starting to hurt Marco's feelings," Petra said when he got back. She cocked an eyebrow at his rumpled and lipstick-smeared appearance.

"Oh, I *ate*," Luke said, waggling his eyebrows and leering comically.

Petra rolled her eyes heavenward. "Give me strength," she said to the ceiling, then glared at him. "Is that all the Ice Queen let you do?"

"Nope," he said cheerfully, refusing to let her sour looks spoil his lingering afterglow. "And let me tell you, that girl's mouth is *glorious*."

"You, my friend, are a pig. Brush your teeth and maybe wash your dirty mind before you see Yuna tomorrow night…. Oh, wait, *tonight*."

"He is seeing that Korean girl today and you do *nothing*?" Helga demanded.

Svetlana smiled Sphinx-like at her matchmaker. "I don't need to. He's already had the little masseuse. Men are fickle creatures. He won't want her again, not after I 'blew his mind', as he put it."

Helga rolled her eyes in exasperation and dealt Svetlana's ass a stinging slap, making her jump. "You put too much stock in your mouth and beauty. You have not won this yet. You must be much, *much* better than all the rest before you get access to his wealth, power, and connections. Remember, the organization does not tolerate failure!"

Svetlana turned on the older woman and slapped her face. "I *never* fail. Remember that." Helga cowered submissively remembering the time that Svetlana had put her in the hospital.

Yuna was bubbling over with excitement. Petra had said that Luke was taking her dancing, and she couldn't help but twirl girlishly in front of the mirror, watching her yellow silk cocktail dress flare.

"I'm glad you are happy, dear one," Roki San said. "I do not know if he has learned what his heart wants yet, but I can see that you have learned what yours wants."

Yuna's smile faded and she looked sadly out the window at the headlights of the approaching limousine. "Yes. I think I *have* fallen in love with him. Am I foolish?"

"No, child, it is never foolish to follow your heart. Perhaps he will find wisdom too, and your heart will not be broken," Roki said, then shooed Yuna towards the door as the doorbell chimes rang throughout the mansion.

Luke took Yuna's hand in his own as she stepped out onto her mansion's porch. "You look beautiful tonight," he said with a genuine smile.

Yuna laughed up at him. "It's a little more glamorous," she said.

"Not the dress. You. You're just glowing," he replied. He took her in his arms and danced a few steps with her. "Let's go dancing."

She giggled at his antics, matching his dancing easily. "I would love to," she said.

Luke felt an odd sort of sweet ache in his chest and hugged her close before leading her to the limousine. He didn't know what it was about this girl. He'd already had her, he should have promptly lost interest; she was no Carla. But here he was, wanting to know everything about her.

"Some of my staff play together in a little band. I think we're their first victims... Um, audience," he said.

Yuna snickered and bumped her shoulder into his upper arm. "They can't be *that* bad. I'm sure you only hire talented people," she said, eyes crinkled with amusement.

"Let's hope for the best? If all else fails, there is a sound system, so I can plug in my cell phone and play some tunes from my playlist," Luke said. *"Why does it make me ridiculously happy when she smiles and laughs at me?"* he thought. "How is your back feeling?" asked Yuna, running her hand lightly over his old injury. "It hasn't felt this good in years!" said Luke, smiling brightly and kissing Yuna on her lush lips.

Their arrival at the gazebo was heralded by a long and intricate drum solo from Petra. Luke shook his head at her, wondering how long she'd been wanting to show *that* off.

Yuna looked around as Luke helped her out of the limo. "Wow! Petra's really good!"

"Just wait 'till you hear the rest of us!" Maximillian called out and joined in with the bass guitar.

"They sound like they've been playing together forever," Yuna said, putting her hand on his offered elbow and walking up the gazebo steps with him.

"Can you play something romantic?" Luke asked them, still skeptical as to whether or not this would actually work out.

"Oh, I think we can manage that just fine. Boys, how about *Blue Moon*?" Petra asked. Luke was delighted to find that they were actually pretty good.

"I love this song," Yuna said as he took her into his arms.

"I like this sort of music for dancing to as well," Luke admitted. "I like a lot of different music. What about you?"

"A little bit of everything. My playlist looks like it was compiled by a hoarder, really," admitted Yuna.

Luke laughed at her self-deprecating expression. "Me too. Petra teases me that since things have started going well that I have no self-control at all about getting more music," he said.

He spontaneously twirled her just as they were hitting a patch of moonlight, which lit her and her dress with a soft glow. *"She looks like an angel,"* he thought. *"No, more like some kind of little fairy creature, all solemn and merry at once. She looks like..."* Luke stopped that train of thought, not wanting to go there.

They danced on through the night and into the wee hours of the morning. It seemed like they talked about everything, but he couldn't think of much beyond the way she fit in his arms so perfectly. He wanted her with a quiet desperation that made him curse himself for having his staff there at all.

It was nearly dawn when he brought her back to her mansion. At the door, he pulled her close and kissed her for what seemed like the thousandth time. At first the kiss was sweet and lingering, but the way she melted into him drove him half-mad.

He lifted her easily and groaned when she wrapped her legs around his waist. He heard a loud throat-clearing and broke the kiss, absurdly pleased at the disappointed whimper she made.

"So sorry," Roki San said from the doorway.

"No, no. I guess I should apologize for acting like a teenager on the porch," Luke said, putting Yuna down, even though it was abundantly clear that she would prefer to have stayed wrapped around him. He gave them both a crooked, boyish grin and ran his hand through his hair, looking appropriately sheepish. Yuna gave him a brilliant smile and he smiled back as he headed back to his limousine.

Chapter 7: Choices

"Took quite a while for you to get back. Should I even ask?" Petra looked up at him from her monitors.

"Got caught making out on the porch," Luke admitted, shaking his head at himself. "It felt like being seventeen caught with my hand up the neighbor girl's skirt."

"You didn't!" Petra squawked, spinning her chair and glaring at him.

"Nah, but if the blasted matchmaker hadn't interrupted when she did I would have had a lot more than my *hand* under her skirt," he said.

"I'll send her flowers for good timing. I've got some preliminary results on the investigation. You should take a look through them before you pick the final two," Petra said, handing him a thumb drive.

"Dammit. That's today?"

"If you hadn't stayed out 'till all hours you might be better prepared," Petra said, rolling her eyes.

"I'm going to sleep on it. If they show up have them check their torches and pitchforks at the door. Anything on this that I should be aware of right away?" Luke held up the drive.

"Not really, just the obvious. It definitely wasn't Dova — but she wouldn't be stupid enough to sabotage herself anyway — and I'm almost positive it wasn't Yuna. She was in camera range for all but about thirty minutes of the whole night, and even that was in a bathroom without a window."

Luke nodded and headed off to his bedroom, kicking his shoes off with a sigh and for a moment seriously considering falling asleep in his Saville Row suit. He popped the thumb drive into the computer and brought the file up to scan through while he got undressed.

He cued up the raw video footage and fell asleep watching Svetlana's matchmaker standing next to a hammock.

His dreams were vivid and nightmarish, his head insisting on running through worst-case scenarios of what would happen in any version of the upcoming choice. Dova would compete with him endlessly and his pleasant morning runs would turn into entering the damned ultra-marathon. Pamela would believe every damned thing printed about him. Kiko would be distant and timid in public and frigid in private. Svetlana would go back to bored and dissatisfied and would only want to talk business when she was even talking to him at all. Yuna would be totally lost at high society functions and possibly be a source of gossip in the tabloids...

Luke woke up, stretching his back and rotating the kink out of his neck. *"Wild ass dreams,"* he thought grouchily. He rifled through his closet and dressed casually, then went looking for Petra and whatever bad news she had for him this time.

When he found her, Petra seemed to be waiting less than patiently for him. "They're in the conference room," she said.

"Any progress on finding out who cut those branches?" he asked.

"Nothing new. I've got a gut feeling, but I can't pin it on any of them," she replied.

Yuna sat in the conference room waiting, twisting her hands together with anxiety, head bowed. She was certain that with her luck, Luke would decide to send her home, just when she'd fallen in love with him.

Pamela reached out and patted her hand. "It will be fine, Yuna dear," she said.

Yuna tried to smile bravely for her friend and nodded.

Luke entered the room with Petra and stuck his hands in his pockets, glaring at them all as if they were a particularly bothersome project that he couldn't figure out. Yuna looked up at him and felt sorrow when looking at his face.

"I trust you have made your decision, Mr. Garmount," Kaito, Kiko's matchmaker, said.

"Yes. It was difficult, but I know what I'm looking for in a companion," Luke said, rocking back and forth on his heels a few times.

"Then stop stalling and tell us," Debra, Dova's matchmaker, said sourly.

Yuna raised sad eyes to Luke. If he was going to tell her to go, she wanted to be looking at him when he did. Their eyes met and Luke looked troubled for just a moment before Petra cleared her throat loudly and nudged his side with an elbow.

"Huh? Oh. Yes. Yuna and Svetlana will stay," Luke said with more coldness than he had wanted.

Yuna's eyes widened with surprise and she smiled up at him, she hadn't expected him to choose her – she wasn't as beautiful as the other girls, at least in her own mind – never mind the sweet, tender smile he gave her.

Pamela started to sob into her matchmaker's shoulder pitifully, true despair in her voice.

Dova sighed and stood. "Not to be sour grapes about the matter, but it's probably for the best. I rather prefer my dates a bit less dangerous," she said, then hobbled out of the room, heavily favoring her uninjured leg.

Kiko was whispering to her matchmaker as they left, ignoring the pained look in Luke's eyes. Pamela followed soon after, also without speaking.

"I'd say no hard feelings, but I think they might lynch me," Luke said quietly to Petra, though Yuna heard him.

Chapter 8: Saying Goodbye

Luke decided that single dates weren't going to cut it this time around. He would spend several days with each of the girls. However, he couldn't decide whether he should move in with each of them, or move them each into his mansion for a few days and then back out again. Moving them both in at the same time was absolutely out of the question – he was *not* going to have two competing women in the same house.

"What do you think? One at a time here or move in with them for a few days each?" Luke gestured in the vague direction of the girls' mansions with the knife he was using to make his sandwich.

"Some peace and quiet to get stuff done work-wise would be nice, so feel free to bring Sven and Maximillian with you. Even though the other women are gone... you still need to play it safe until we find out who cut those tree branches," Petra said, then smiled impishly. "The last thing I need is to lose my hero boss before he can buy me a mansion on the beach!"

"Yeah. You're right... as usual. I already put in a room for me in each of the mansions, so I won't need *everything*. How soon can the staff have some basics packed?" Luke asked, pouring himself a cup of coffee.

"Give them an hour – longer if you want to bring that speed demon computer of yours," she said.

"Nah. I think the girls will be plenty entertaining all by themselves," he said, grinning lasciviously.

Petra rolled her eyes and picked up her cell phone to get the staff working on packing out the essentials. "How long are you going to be with each of them?" she asked, covering the mic on her phone for a moment.

"A week with each of them, I think. That ought to be enough time to get to know them as well as I'll ever need to," Luke said. He leaned back a little on the kitchen stool and took a satisfied sip of his coffee. *This is all working out!* he thought. *"You can't beat The Bullet!"*

###

"Still you are not first in his mind! He will be here in minutes, expecting to spend a week in your company. You must mesmerize him or the Korean girl will take you from his mind," Helga, Svetlana's matchmaker, said.

Svetlana nodded, then spread her satin robe to reveal the daring lingerie beneath. "I think," Svetlana said, "that he will be suitably enthralled."

"Do not imagine that a man of his wealth will be taken in by nothing more than your body. Mr. Garmount didn't get rich by inheritance... he is no fool! He can bathe in gold coins like a dragon, he will look for more than beauty," Helga said warningly.

###

Luke arrived well after the staff had already set up his things in the room he had designed to be his own when he had the girls' mansions built.

"Hi, Honey! I'm home!" he called out from the doorway when he saw Svetlana on the landing at the top of the main staircase.

She laughed, tied the sash of her satin robe, and descended the stairs toward him at a sedate pace. She seemed entirely assured that his eyes would be solely on her, and she wasn't wrong. Luke's eyes were glued to the tantalizing glimpses of her long legs, peeping out of the shimmering black satin gown.

34

"So good to see you again. I have instructed the staff to prepare a light dinner, if you would care to eat," Svetlana said, kissing him lightly on each cheek before stepping back and running a finger down the edge of her robe. "Although... Perhaps you are not so hungry?"

Luke swept her up into his arms and headed for the stairs. "Chucking leftovers in the microwave sounds like a plan to me," he said, chuckling at her gasps of alarm as he bounded up the stairs in no time.

In the hall, she pointed towards her room rather than the room where his belongings had been unpacked. He carried her in and kicked the door closed behind him, though it didn't shut all the way, catching just slightly on the thick white carpeting. He slid his Italian leather loafers off and padded across the floor, nibbling on her neck as he walked.

He headed straight for her bed, tossing her onto it and following immediately, capturing her mouth in a heated kiss. He leaned back briefly, untying her robe's sash to find the lovely present hidden within. His eyes widened with delight when he saw the crotch-less black satin teddy. She rose up to meet him with another searing kiss, unbuttoning his shirt as he unbuckled his belt.

He threw his clothes to the floor and stripped the robe off of her, adding them to the pile with his shoes. In seconds they were naked. Luke grabbed her hips and pulled her to the edge of the bed.

Svetlana hooked her legs around his waist and pulled him close. "I want you so bad," she said as she slowly pulled him closer her.

Luke rocked against her, pressing his length against her teasingly, delighting in how very wet and ready for him she was. "I was just thinking the same thing," he said, his voice a low, sexy rumble.

She gave him a sultry look from under her lashes and caressed her breasts. "So take me," she said, nearly purring.

He leaned back and then pushed into her. She was snug, but after just a moment he was deep inside her. He straightened, holding her hips, only her shoulders and head still touching the bed, and began thrusting into her.

Svetlana moaned loudly, clutching the duvet with her tightly balled fists. Her legs wrapped still tighter around his waist, pulling him in even deeper while she squeezed his massive girth. Her cries grew louder as he sped up, driving her towards an easy orgasm that seemed to last forever.

Helga stepped out of the house. She was sure that Svetlana had purposefully left the door to her bedroom open, showing off that she had 'caught' the rich man. She shook her head and pressed the transmitter in the watch she had lifted from the girl's room.

"Get here, bring back up. Your very stupid operative thinks she has the prize just because she's got him in her bed," she said coldly.

Chapter 9: Schemes

Luke couldn't quite put his finger on it, but he just couldn't seem to capture the euphoric happiness he felt with Yuna when he was with Svetlana. The week he spent with her was largely spent either being bored out of his mind, irritated by her prying into his business affairs, or having incredible sex.

He elected to walk to Yuna's to clear his head with some fresh air. He had to think about this rationally. Svetlana was great in bed and would look magnificent on his arm, a true trophy, but something inside him felt hollow, no matter how merrily she laughed at his corny jokes. He sighed and walked on, wondering what he was supposed to do. He wanted a companion, someone who would do just what Svetlana did – look good and fuck like a champ, and *not* creep into his heart.

Luke knocked on Yuna's door and was greeted by her smiling face moments later. She wrapped her arms around his waist in an impulsive hug, and he marveled at how good it felt just to have her hold him tight as he hugged her back.

"I didn't see headlights – what a wonderful surprise!" Yuna said, snuggling into him.

"I'll have to sneak up on you more often if this is your reaction," Luke replied, running a hand over her long, silken black hair.

"Oh, you definitely will – it gives me an excuse!" Yuna giggled and gave him another squeeze before walking into the mansion with him.

He noticed that the furniture had been moved around a bit since the tour he'd taken with the interior designer he'd hired. It felt more welcoming and somehow homier, without being less elegant. He looked down at Yuna and thought that her new decoration choices fit her as well. She was, if anything, just as beautiful as Svetlana in her own way, but she managed to make him feel like he belonged here with her.

###

"He's been at the girl's house for his week. He'll be choosing me tomorrow," Svetlana said, flicking her platinum blonde hair over her shoulder while glaring at Helga and the two Russian Mafia thugs who had met them in the cove at the northern end of the island.

"This I doubt. Tomorrow you and your associates will go to the girl's house. Take the girl, her ridiculous matchmaker, and all of their personal belongings. Make it look like she left of her own volition. *I* leave nothing to chance," Helga snapped.

###

On the last night of his week with Yuna, Luke chased her through the house, both of them soaking wet from another Jacuzzi bath for two. He caught sight of her glorious naked ass and stream of long black hair while heading for the kitchen and heard her wild giggles as he stalked her with leonine grace.

"I give! I give! No tickling!" Yuna said, eyes lit with merriment, clutching her sides protectively.

He picked her up and put her on the counter, then pulled her face close and kissed her. "What about tickling your fancy?" he asked, leering up at her when he broke the kiss.

She gave him the sassy smile he'd grown to enjoy so much in the past week, wrapped her legs around his waist and her arms around his neck. "Well, that's a different story, isn't it? I rather fancy *that* kind of tickling."

Luke laughed delightedly and hugged her close, then picked her up and pelted down the hall and up the stairs to the room that was a replica of his own, which she had informed him she liked just as much, if not more, than hers. She giggled in his ear and let out a delighted whoop when he spun them both around and collapsed backward onto his bed.

Yuna sat up, straddling him and bit her lip, looking at him with clear invitation as she wriggled against him. He lifted his hips, making her squeak when his cock, trapped between them, pressed against her. The sound of her voice was so delicious that he grabbed hold of her and flipped her over doggy style. He slid home, though she was still so tight that he had to take it a little slow.

Yuna sighed contentedly. "You feel so good," she said, pushing her hips backward to meet him.

Luke teased her, sliding almost all the way out despite her attempts to get closer to him, then back in as slow as he could bear, wanting to make this last night last as long as he possibly could.

She made needy sounds, whimpering and whispering his name, getting louder as he ground against her. He grabbed large hanks of her hair, which she loved and pulled tightly. Her first orgasm took hold and nearly drove him over the edge, but he held on, gentling her, kissing her neck and soothing her until she started moving against him again.

"You feel fantastic, baby," Luke said, turning her around, gathering her into his arms and getting to his knees. Once he had her straddling his lap, still deep inside her, he leaned her back, further and further until her shoulders were back on the bed again. He knew this angle would feel amazing for both of them. He pressed the palm of his hand against her pubic bone to hit her G-spot from both sides and rubbed his thumb gently against her clit.

Yuna nearly levitated off the bed with the force of her second orgasm, sitting up and grabbing his ass to get as much of his cock into her as she possibly could, riding him with wild abandon, calling his name out in breathless gasps. No matter how much he wanted to make this last, she felt like heaven and he was ready to go there. She brought him there... like she always did! *This girl is magical*" thought Luke happily as he gave a few more contented thrusts then slowly pulled out of her.

Luke held her close on his lap for a moment before laying her down gently and cuddling up beside her. He slowly ran his hand over her beautiful body, propped up on one elbow to enjoy the dazed expression on her face.

"What's this say?" he asked, tracing a finger over the tattoo just under her navel.

Yuna made a few incoherent sounds, blinked and looked. "It says prosperity and fertility," she said.

Luke's sleep was fitful at best, and he woke the next day ready to choose Svetlana. He couldn't possibly choose Yuna. She clearly wanted a family, and he didn't want to spoil that for her. He smiled fondly, thinking that Yuna would be an amazing mother, then shook his head. No, definitely no love and marriage for him, no house full of gadget-happy little boys and button-bright little girls. He nodded to himself as he walked toward his own mansion. He'd get some sleep and then tell the girls his choice.

Chapter 10: Trapped!

Yuna wept quietly after she closed the door behind Luke. She had seen the way his heart closed to her when she told him what her tattoo said. She was sure that he would send her away and she would never see the man she loved again.

"Hush, now, child. All is not lost," Roki San, Yuna's matchmaker, said gently.

"I... I spoiled *everything*. He doesn't want a family, children, any of it!" Yuna wailed, sobbing into Roki's shoulder.

While the tears were still wet on her face the door opened and four men in dark clothes burst into the mansion, brandishing AK-47s. The two women were quickly surrounded. One of the men used zip ties to secure their hands behind their backs while another gagged them with lengths of black cloth.

"Yuri, gather all of their belongings, every last bead and bauble. The luggage too. Make it look like they left in a hurry, but took everything with them," the largest man said to one of the men behind Yuna. "When you are done, go up to this rich man's mansion and disable his cars."

Yuna looked up at one of the hidden cameras that she had managed to spot with wide, pleading eyes, hoping that Petra was actually watching her monitors despite the early hour.

"Move, you Korean whores," another man said, prodding them each in the back in turn.

Yuna and her matchmaker were marched out of the mansion, and once they were outside, bags were tied over their heads and they were spun around until they were dizzy and unable to guess where they might be headed.

Yuna tried to keep track of what the ground felt like beneath her feet, but she lost hope when she was picked up and dumped unceremoniously into what felt like a small boat. She was terrified, but relaxed slightly when she felt Roki's arm against her own. At least they were together – though she wouldn't have wished this on her elderly friend.

"Ivan! Row to the grotto." Yuna thought that had to be the largest of the men speaking again since he had given the other man, Yuri, orders as well.

The time crept by. Yuna tried to guess how far they were going by the number of sweeps of the oars she heard, but she was unsure how far each stroke took them, particularly in light of Ivan's continuous muttering in Russian.

"Why would Russians kidnap us?" she asked herself. She hated thinking poorly of anyone, but it only made sense that *somehow* Svetlana had arranged for this to happen to ensure her win. That wasn't a terribly comforting thought since there was no ransom to motivate these men to keep them alive.

It might have been a half hour or it might have been three hours, but eventually Yuna felt the little boat run aground on something, and she was picked up and handed off to someone else, then carried. She had no idea where she was, but what little sunlight there had been was no longer warm against her skin and she shivered in the damp darkness. She was tossed down roughly, the back of her head hitting a rock wall behind her with a painful crack. She heard another thump beside her seconds later.

"You stay put," a man's voice said.

Luke tried to get to sleep, to catch up on the rest he hadn't gotten while dwelling on what Yuna really wanted out of life. He tossed and turned, twisting the sheets around himself. He was going to choose Svetlana. Except... Why? With Yuna, he felt happy, whole, content, and warm in a part of his heart he hadn't thought would ever feel again. With Svetlana, he just felt colder and lonelier than ever.

But Yuna obviously wanted marriage and children. He didn't know if he could give those to her. He had been sure – going into this – that those were the very last things he wanted. He didn't want love. He didn't want his heart ripped out again. He had just wanted a companion to be around for social things and to have sex with on a regular basis. It seemed like everything he'd thought he wanted he couldn't have with Yuna.

He sighed and gave up on getting any sleep. Luke got up and put on a pair of swimming briefs, thinking that a swim might help clear his head. He shook his head and left his room. There was no clearing it. He had fallen in love with Yuna, that was all there was to it.

"Boss!" Sven was rounding the corner with a small man in dark clothes wearing handcuffs dangling limply from one of his massive fists.

"What the hell?" Luke asked when the man started struggling frantically to get away from Sven's mighty grip.

"I caught this son-of-a-bitch doing your Lambo dirty. He'd already got the rest of the cars," Sven said as he bounced the man's head off the woodwork to calm him down.

Luke felt rage coursing through him and stepped forward, getting face-to-face with the saboteur. "Why the fuck were you messing with my cars?" He didn't give the man a chance to answer, instead roaring and elbowing him in the face hard enough to break his already-ugly nose. Luke usually had more self-control...

Petra raced down the hallway toward them at top speed. "I just went through this morning's footage and this guy and a bunch of his friends grabbed Yuna and her matchmaker and made off with them," Petra said, gasping.

"Who the fuck sent you?" Luke asked, rounding on the bleeding thug Sven held against the wall.

The thug hawked and tried to spit in Luke's face, but Luke was too quick, giving him a merciless punch to the stomach. After a few breathless seconds the man gasped: "Fuck you," in a Russian accent thick and gluey from his recently broken nose.

Sven bounced the guy's head off the wall hard enough to knock him out and leave a dent in the woodwork. "You don't need a murder rap," Sven said with a shrug when Luke glared at him.

"If his buddies harm so much as one *hair* on her head...," Luke growled menacingly, his adrenaline pumping.

"Look, get that scheming bitch, Svetlana, here... Now!" said Petra. "Make like you're going to choose her if you have to. Just get her here and we'll find out where they took Yuna. That's way more important."

Chapter 11: Riding to the Rescue

Svetlana and her matchmaker, Helga, walked into the mansion. Sven and Maximillian stepped up from either side of the door and grabbed them. Both women fought back, but Helga's KGB training made her the more formidable opponent.

As Sven struggled to hold on to Svetlana, Marco charged out of the kitchen brandishing a cast iron skillet and smacked it into the back of Helga's head, causing her to collapse into a heap at Maximillian's feet.

"Thanks for the assist," Maximillian said, picking the older woman up.

"Couldn't have my bass player wreck his hands. Besides, word got around. Yuna's a sweet girl, she don't deserve this," Marco said, his Long Island accent thicker with his outrage. "Lemme brain the blonde bitch and we'll be even."

Petra stepped forward with two pairs of handcuffs, handing them to the bodyguards.

"Remind me not to ask why you have those when this is finished," Luke said, shaking his head at his longtime assistant. He turned to Svetlana and growled in her face, "The deal's off, and you're going to tell me where the hell Yuna is."

"Why should I? Maybe I will have her killed to spite you," Svetlana said, eyes narrowing dangerously.

"Petra," Luke said, radiating fury, "call Interpol. Now. Sven, Max, toss them in the freezer with their little friend. Svetlana, you can just hope that freezer isn't as airtight as advertised, right?"

"Let us all go and I'll tell you where she is," Svetlana bargained, digging in her heels and trying to resist.

"Why should I let *any* of you go?" Luke asked.

"Because if I don't report to them in less than an hour, the others will kill your little Korean whore," Svetlana spat.

"You tell me where she is, I get her back, and then I *might* let you go before Interpol gets here," Luke said, crossing his arms over his broad chest and glaring at her with the full fury of a Greek God in his prime.

"Fine! Fine, yes, go get her. Why not, they're heavily armed men. Stupid American. They're in the grotto on the southern tip of the island. Go on, get shot. Once you're dead, your pretty little island paradise will make a perfect base of operations for smuggling, even if I *don't* get my hands on your money," Svetlana said vehemently, kicking at Luke's groin. Luke easily blocked the shot and then instantly bitch slapped her on instinct across the face... hard.

Put them both in the freezer. Now," said Luke, making an imperious motion with his hands. Luke followed his bodyguards, grimly satisfied by Svetlana's desperate look when the freezer door slammed in her face.

"How the hell are we going to get down there in less than an hour? The cars are all out of commission!" Sven said.

"Horses," Petra said. "You okay to ride, boss-man?"

"For the woman I love, I'd do anything!," Luke replied, striding out the French doors to the patio, determined to reach the little barn that held his horses as quickly as possible and a little surprised at his declaration of love for Yuna.

Petra let out a joyous whoop that earned her a swift glare from her employer. "What? I knew you'd fall for one of them," she said, keeping pace with him.

"We're bringing the heavy firepower, boss, you stay behind us and wear this," Maximillian said, handing Luke a fully bulletproof vest, trousers and helmet along with an enhanced AK-47 with armor piercing bullets.

Luke took it and quickly put it on. "I'm getting Yuna out of there, not hanging behind. Give me those extra clips," he said.

Yuna heard nothing but the sound of the surf for what seemed like hours. She sat with her ankle touching Roki San's – that little bit of contact was all the comfort she had. She didn't know if Luke would even realize that she was gone, and helpless tears tracked down her cheeks, soaking the gag still in her mouth.

She lifted her head, hearing something different. Arguing? There was shouting, but far enough away that she couldn't understand anything beyond the anger in the tones.

There was loud popping sounds, and before she could figure out what it was, Roki San had launched herself sideways, knocking both of them over, her frail old body protecting Yuna. The sounds of gunfire continued, very fast and frantic.

"Oh no! Luke! Oh, don't be firing at Luke! Let him be safe!" Yuna thought desperately.

The gunfire grew louder, and there was more shouting, this time in Russian. Something hit the stone wall above Yuna's head and she could feel shards of rock falling, cutting into her skin, and she was sure that Roki was getting it much worse.

There were several minutes of gunfire... more shouting, more noise, getting louder and louder... almost deafening now. Yuna could feel heavy things hitting the sand near her. She wanted to scream but remained silent. More thuds, rhythmic – running feet? Hands lifted Roki off of her and lifted her up. She whimpered in fear, not knowing if the Russians had won the shootout or not.

The bag was lifted off of her head and she saw Luke's face lit by the reflection of the water in the mouth of the cave. He pulled a knife from his belt and sawed away at the zip ties holding her hands behind her back, then gently removed the gag from her mouth before gathering her into his arms and rocking back and forth with her as she sobbed into his shoulder.

"I thought I'd lost you," Luke said, his voice muffled by her hair. "I never want to lose you, Yuna. I love you."

Yuna leaned back, shocked, looking into his eyes to see the truth of his words shining out at her. "I love *you*, Luke. I was so scared I would never get a chance to tell you," she said.

"Tell me every day for the rest of our lives. Marry me. Today? Tomorrow? I don't care, but soon," he said, then laughed at her renewed shock.

"You want to marry me? Yes! Oh, of *course*! Yes, yes, I'll marry you!" Yuna babbled, tears of happiness streaming down her face, throwing her arms around Luke's neck.

"That's a lovely proposal, but I cannot applaud wisdom finally finding you until someone sets me free," Roki San said, holding up her tied hands as Luke quickly cut her free.

###

When Interpol finally arrived three days later, they were hurriedly handed six very bruised and beat up prisoners by Luke's overdressed staff. None of the Russians had died, but several had come damn close. Whether it was Luke who had shot them or one of his bodyguards... for official purposes it was the massive Maxmillian and Sven who had taken the credit for that. Once the prisoners were secured in the first helicopter, the remaining agents headed for the sound of voices on the beach to debrief those responsible for the capture of the Russian gangsters.

###

After Luke's close call with death... several of the Russian bullets had whizzed just by his head, he had decided that it was far past time for him to truly enjoy his life. The first thing Luke did was give Yuna's matchmaker, Roki, a large check for more than the deal required, 50 million dollars, and a first class ticket back to her home in South Korea. Luke then spared no expense to wine and dine his beautiful Yuna. After six months on the island, Yuna expressed a desire to head home to visit her family. Luke smiled at her playfully then said: "There is only one way that you are ever going to leave this island." Luke then got on one knee and pulled out a massive, perfectly cut diamond ring. "And that's as my wife." Looking up at Yuna, Luke smiled. "Yuna, you have taught me what it is like to love again. I hadn't realized how broken I was until I thought that I might lose you forever. I love you with all my heart and soul. Will you marry me?" Yuna's heart melted and her eyes filled with tears. "Of course" she said simply, with that magical sing song tone her voice that Luke had grown to love. Luke placed the diamond on her finger then stood up and kissed her passionately under the moonlit sky. In the history of the world, there have been a few kisses that have truly been able to transcend space and time... and this one beautiful and passionate kiss left them all behind.

My Other Books and Audio Books

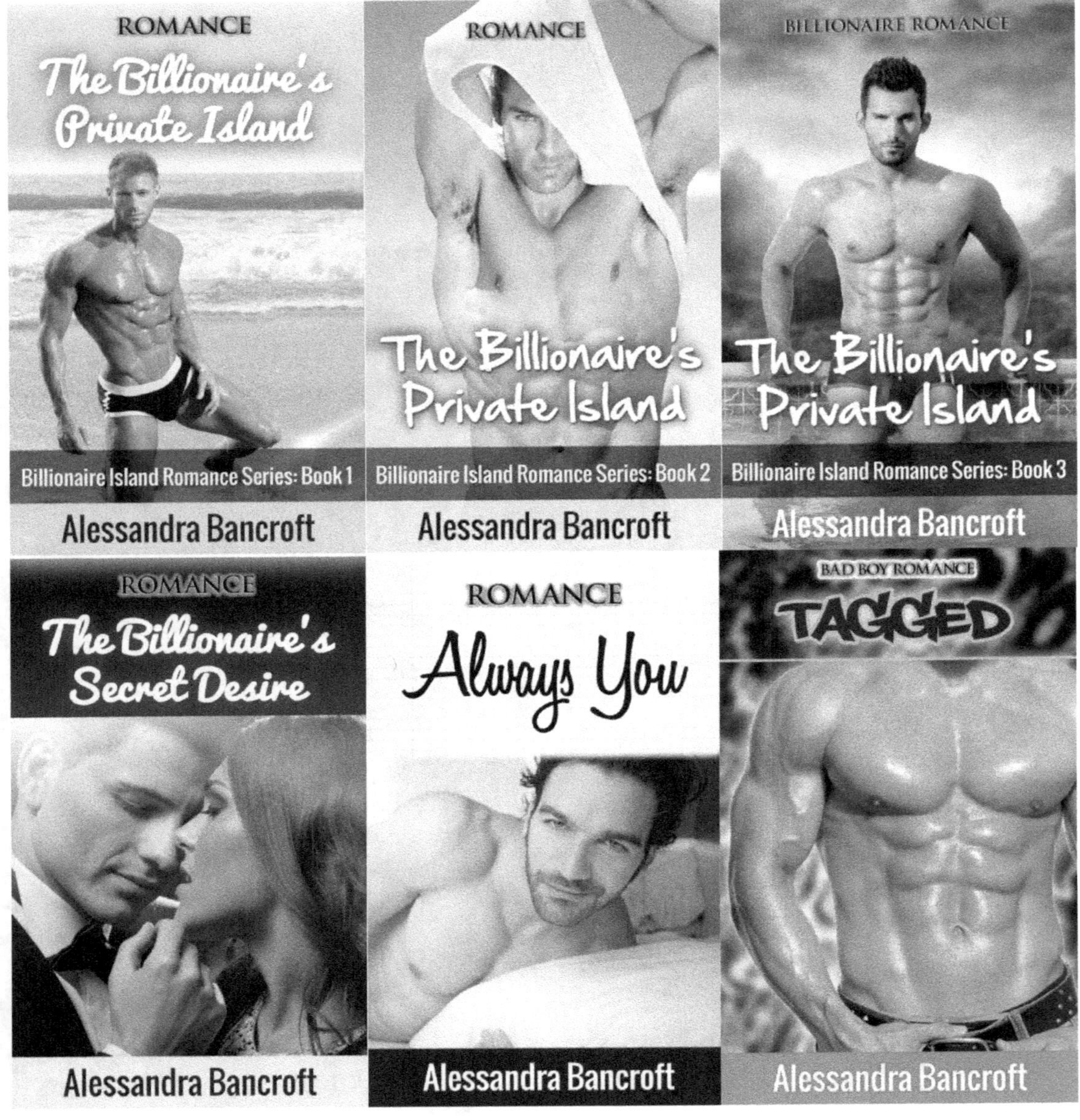

All of these are available in audio book as well.

***If you enjoyed this book then please spare a few seconds to easily post a quick positive review. It would be greatly appreciated!**†*

Thanks for reading.